Diary of a Wombat

by Jackie French

illustrated by Bruce Whatley

sandpiper

Houghton Mifflin Harcourt
Boston   New York

To Mothball, and all others.
J.F.

Thanks for letting me play, Jackie. This was fun.
B.W.

Text copyright © 2002, 2003 by Jackie French
Illustrations copyright © Farmhouse Illustration Company Pty Limited 2002

First published in Australia in 2002 by Angus & Robertson, an imprint of Harper Collins Publishers, Australia.
Published in the United States in 2003.

The illustrations were executed in acrylic paints.
The text was set in Kid's Stuff Plain.

www.hmhco.com

Library of Congress Cataloging-in-Publication Data

French, Jackie.
Diary of a wombat / written by Jackie French ; illustrated by Bruce Whatley.
p.   cm.
Summary: In its diary, wombat describes life of eating, sleeping and getting to know some new human neighbors.
HC ISBN-13: 978-0-618-38136-4   PA ISBN-13: 978-0-547-07669-0
[1. Wombats—Fiction. 2. Diaries—Fiction.] I. Whatley, Bruce, ill. II. Title.
PZ7.F88903Di 2003
[E]— dc21   2003000829

Manufactured in China
SCP 20 19 18 17 16 15
4500799394

I'm a wombat. I live in Australia.

As you can see from my picture,

I look a little like a bear, but smaller.

I live in a hole in the ground.

I come out mostly at night,

and during the day I sleep.

I eat grass and roots and, of course,

the occasional treat . . .

Monday

Morning: Slept.

Afternoon: Slept.

Evening: Ate grass.

Scratched.

Night: Ate grass.

Slept.

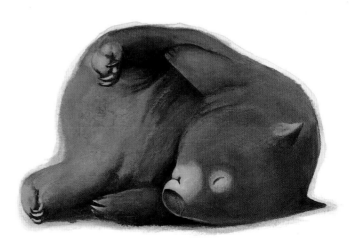

Tuesday

Morning: Slept.

Afternoon: Slept.

Evening: Ate grass.

Night: Ate grass. Decided grass is boring.

Scratched. Hard to reach the itchy bits.

Slept.

Wednesday

Morning: Slept.

Afternoon: Mild, cloudy day.

I have new neighbors. Humans!

Found the perfect dustbath.

Discovered flat, hairy creature
invading my territory.

Fought major battle with
flat, hairy creature.

Won battle.
Neighbors should be pleased.

Demanded a reward.

Received a carrot.
It was delicious.

Evening: Demanded more carrots.

No response.

Chewed hole in door.

FOR PETE'S SAKE, GIVE HER SOME CARROTS!

Ate carrots.

Scratched.

Went to sleep.

Thursday

Morning: Slept.

Afternoon:

Discovered the perfect scratching post.

Evening: Demanded carrots.

No response.

Tried yesterday's hole.

Curiously resistant to my paws.

Banged on large metal object
till carrots appeared.

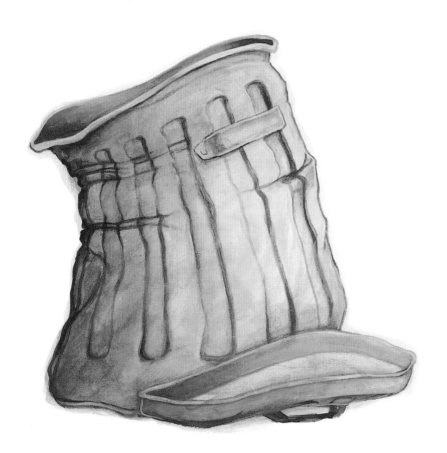

Ate carrots.

Began new hole in soft dirt.

Went to sleep.

Friday

Morning: Slept.

Afternoon: Discovered new
scratching post.

Also discovered a new
source of carrots.

Evening: Someone has filled in my new hole.

Soon dug it out again.

Night: Worked on hole.

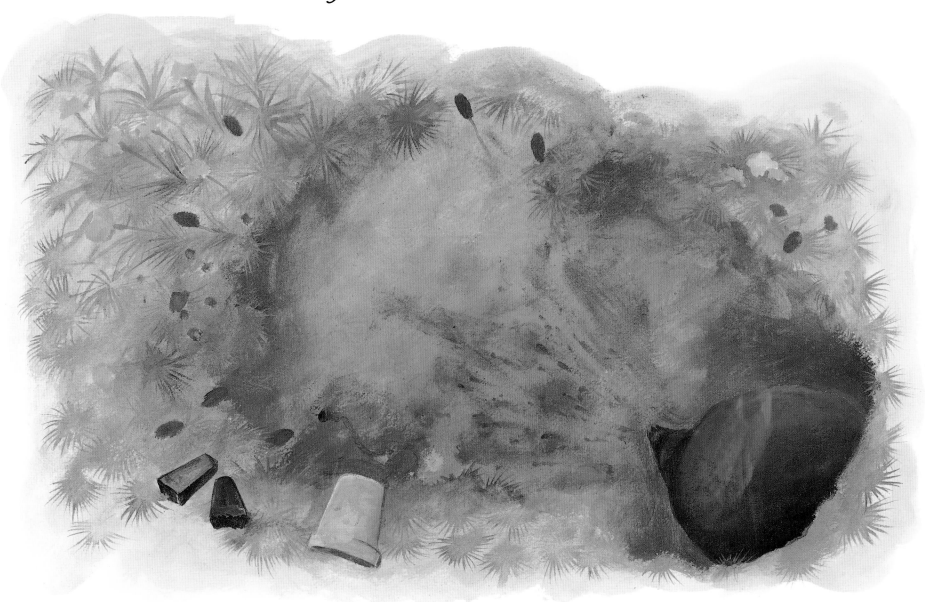

Saturday

Morning: Moved into new hole.

Afternoon: Rained.

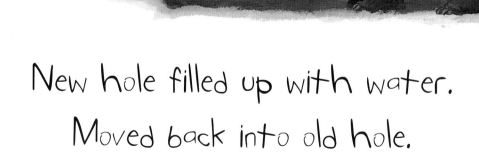

New hole filled up with water.

Moved back into old hole.

Evening: Discovered even more carrots.
Never knew there were so many carrots in the world.
Carrots delicious.

Night: Finished carrots.

Slept.

Sunday

Morning: Slept.

Afternoon: Slept

Evening: Slept

Night: Was offered carrots at the back door.

Decided carrots are boring.

Chewed a few things.

Didn't like any of them.

Demanded something other than carrots.

Received bowl of oats.

Ate oats.

Monday

Morning: Slept.

Afternoon: Felt energetic.
Wet things flapped against
my nose on my way to the back door.

Got rid of them.

Demanded oats AND carrots.
Only had to bang large metal object
for a short time before they appeared.

Evening: Have decided that humans
are easily trained and make quite good pets.

Night: Dug new hole
to be closer to them.

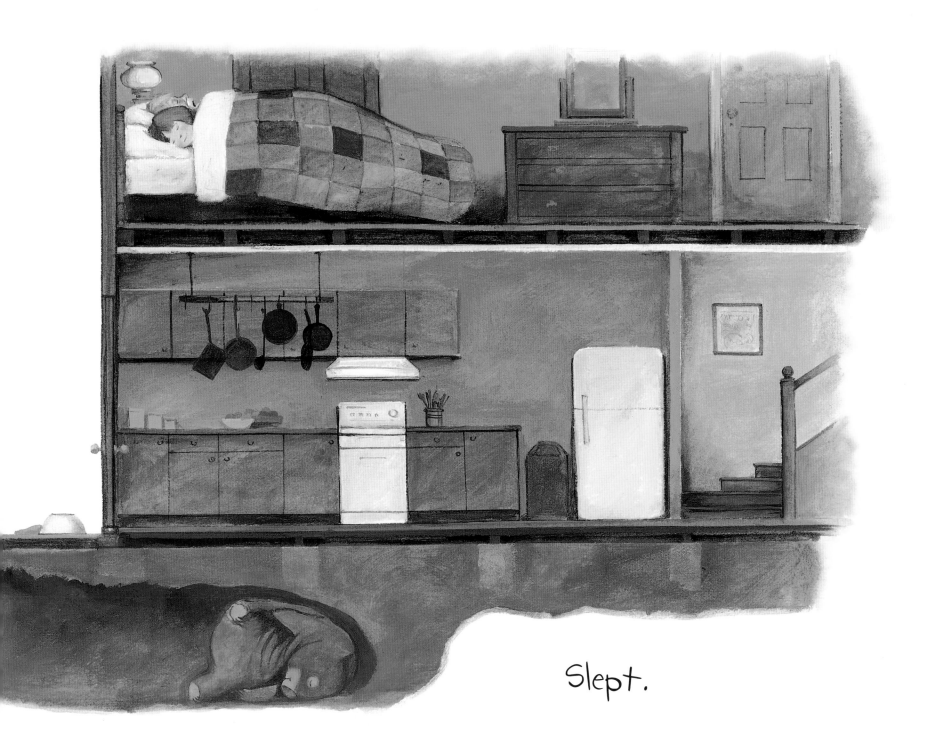

Slept.